AKBAR – BIRBAL STORIES COLOR

MR VIVEK KUMAR PANDEY SHAMBHUNATH

ISBN 979-888569130-7

Disclaimer : During Writing This Book No character & No religious , No Relation Members Are Harmed. It's Only For Study & Entertainment Purpose. Do Not Take Seriously,Written By Mr Vivek Kumar Pandey.

Contents

Contents

Foreword

In This Book There Is 40+ Story Of Akbar - Birbal in English Language. During Writing This Book No Character And No Religion Are Harmed. It's Only For Study Purpose. Written By Mr Vivek Kumar Pandey. winner youngest writer award 1st rank in india 2020.He is only one writer can publish 830 + own book that was greatest successfull in his life.This All Credit Goes To My Super Hero Daddy. This book fully colour Edition.

Preface

Author biography in English :MY NAME IS VIVEK KUMAR PANDEY . I WAS BORN IN 30 SEP 2002,I AM FROM SURAT GUJARAT INDIA.MY DREAM WAS TO BE GOOD WRITERS ,MY FAMILY SUPPORTED ME TO SUCCESSFUL AND I CAN DO IT MY SELF.How do I write? That is a question, I believe, that can be honestly answered by me."CELEBRATING YOUNGEST WRITER AWARD WINNER IN GUJARAT 1ST RANK" MR PANDEY JI . I may think I did a good job writing something . The reader is the one who decides the quality of my writing. I do find writing to be natural to me and therefore find it to be a real challenge. My trick as a challenged writer is to do the best I can and know that I am happy with the final outcome. It may take a while to do my best and there may be quite a few problems I run into along the way.

I am not a greedy person those who are thinking about me and my self I never tried it anyone people suffering from sadness ,I trying to get promoted people suffering from happiness and joy in your Life Time. Now in current situation in India and also world people are unemployed and have no many but our indian governor help to people to get free food from ration card , i also take part in leadership team ,i am Motivational speaker , Film script writer. There was my two dream firstly writer and secondly actor & also my own film is upcoming soon i done almost completely completed script for my film .I AM GOING TO SAY WORD OF HEART TOUCH OUT PLEASE READ IT" , firstly i thanks my father he supports me in this field they always getting inspired me by own his words and behavior ,they always said that he was a biggest person in the world in future and also they purchase fruit and chocolate for me in anytime & anyway , firstly my father buy him then call me Vivek you want a chocolate i will say yes papa but how many tell me ,papa: you tell me how much i buy him i told 1 or 2 chocolate but my father purchase whole the boxes of chocolate and they get suprised me. MY FATHER WAS BORN IN " 20 SEPTEMBER" 1971 IN INDIA.

1) MY FATHER FAVORITE CLOTHES IS KURTA PAIJMA AND ALSO STYLES SHOE

2) FAVORITE SINGER IS KISHORE DA

3) FAVORITE STATE GUJARAT AND KOLKATA , HIS VILLAGE IN BIHAR

4) FAVORITE COLOR BLACK AND WHITE

THEY ALSO LOVE cricket like IPL and one day t-20 .they also like watching a News daily and heard the song daily ,they also interested in tik tok video but in current time tik tok is banned in india but also few videos are in you tube. In lockdown time my family and me very enjoy day daily. my father play daily ludo with his sister and son, daughter.they always loved tea and coffee anytime call me "। वविक थोडा़ चाय बनाओना वविक तमु्हारे हाथ का चाय अच्छा लगता है". I make it tea for my father but some reason after the April to june they are suffering from fever and cough , weakness on 6 June 2020 my father death. they not told me say bye bye his life. After death of 6 June on 10 june my mom and dad anniversary.but my father is Best in the world they can do anything for me please take care of father and respect it of your parents.

CHAPTER ONE

Ch : 1 Mughal Empire

- Ch : 1 Mughal Empire

Akbar was one of the greatest emperors of the Mughal dynasty. It was during the reign of Akbar that the rule of the Mughals truly began, for both Babur and Humayun had ruled for extremely short and interrupted periods.

Akbar was a minor at the time of his father's death, and was under the guardianship of Bairam Khan. Soon after succeeding to the throne Akbar had to firmly establish Mughal authority and regain the territories it had lost. His enemies challenged his rule and another historic battle was fought at Panipat, one in which Akbar emerged victorious and firmly established the Mughal power as the dominant power in India.

Akbar was still under the guardianship of Bairam but now wished to become a full fledged king in his own right. Bairam while providing invaluable service had begun behaving in a high handed manner which had resulted in many enemies.

In 1560 Akbar expressed his desire to take over, to Bairam, who reluctantly agreed and prepared to leave the empire. Akbar made the tactical mistake of appointing Pir Muhammad, an enemy of Bairam's to oversee his move out of Mughal territory. Bairam considered this an insult and rose against Akbar. He was however defeated but allowed to continue out of the empire by Akbar, because of the tremendous services he had rendered. Tragically however Bairam was killed by an Afghan who held a personal grudge against him.

Luckily his family escaped and his son Abdur Rahim was taken in by Akbar and rose later on to become an important noble of the empire. After assuming control from Bairam Akbar did not immediately get full control of the empire. His foster mother Maham Anaga and her son Adam Khan and some of her family were exercising an undue influence on the state.

Adam Khan led some conquests which although successful were brutal. Akbar unable to tolerate their actions put Adam Khan to death in 1562. His foster mother died of grief forty days later. Akbar at the young age of fourteen was now finally in control of his empire.Akbar began a process of consolidation and expansion. He extended the empire's frontiers and they covered almost the entire country, even reaching deep into the south.

< He set up the Mughal administration, drawing heavily on the institutions and concepts that Sher Shah had used. Under Akbar the Mughal empire reached its peak, with its influence extending to almost all parts of the country as well as major developments taking place in the arts and the economy. Akbar ruled for a period of 51 years which was the longest reign amongst the Mughal emperors.

Akbar was one of the most able rulers amongst the Mughals and one of the greatest emperors in Indian history. Akbar was a very wise and open minded ruler with a sound character. He was an able administrator as well as a capable soldier. He possesed tremendous courage, often risking his life and was also extremely strong. He was kind and just and despite being a great conqueror he was not cruel to those whom he had defeated. Akbar was not vengeful and usually forgave people who rebelled against him,except in certain cases when it was not possible.

Akbar possessed tremendous self control and had excellent manners. He is said to have been very charming and was praised by all those who came into contact with him. Akbar had a wise and able courtier called Birbal, and there are many stories about the interactions between Akbar and Birbal, who would often provide sound insights into the various problems the emperor was facing.

Akbar was also very popular amongst his subjects who considered him not only the ruler of Delhi but of the entire universe. Akbar also closely monitored his diet and ate moderately.

While Akbar did not know how to read and write, one cannot say that he was not a learned man. He had a keen interest in literature and philosophy and was gifted with a brilliant mind and incredible memory. He maintained a large library of books and engaged people to read books to him.

His understanding of what he heard was so great that it was said that he could talk so effortlessly on those subjects that one could never get the impression that he was illiterate. Akbar was also a keen patron of art and architecture and many such works flourished in his time.

Akbar was extremely tolerant to religion evident in the fact that he married a Hindu princess. He realized that it was foolish to ill-treat Hindus who formed a majority in his empire.

He made significant efforts to treat them at par and soon they too were being appointed to high posts. Akbar treated religion with an extremely open mind and spent a lot of time studying the various beliefs of the different religions. This eventually resulted in the creation of a new religion of his own called Din-I-illahi .

This combined features from various religions and stressed on the idea of that regardless of what religion you follow, God is one. Being a supreme believer in universal tolerance, Akbar made no attempt to force people to convert to his religion but tried to appeal to the inner feelings of each person.

Akbar's last years brought great grief to him. A beloved friend and notable poet Faizi died in 1595. Akbar's son Salim (later to be known as Jehangir) eager to take over the throne set himself up as an independent king and began plotting to overthrow Akbar. Salim caused much pain to his father when he got another close friend and poet, Abul Fazl murdered. Father and son spent the last couple of years see- sawing between peace and war but finally after Akbar died a natural death, Salim succeeded to the throne. Akbar was a great person and a great king. During his time the country reached a level of prosperity it had not seen and would not see for a long time. Being an able statesmen, he set an example for the other leaders that would follow.

There are many stories about the interactions between Akbar and Birbal, who would often provide sound insights into the various problems the emperor was facing. Akbar was also very popular amongst his subjects who considered him not only the ruler of Delhi but of the entire universe. Akbar also closely monitored his diet and ate moderately. While Akbar did not know how to read and write, one cannot say that he was not a learned man. He had a keen interest in literature and philosophy and was gifted with a brilliant mind and incredible memory. He maintained a large library of books and engaged people to read books to him. His understanding of what he heard was so great that it was said that he could talk so effortlessly on those subjects that one could never get the impression that he was illiterate. Akbar was also a keen patron of art and architecture and many such works flourished in his time.

Akbar was extremely tolerant to religion evident in the fact that he married a Hindu princess. He realized that it was foolish to ill-treat Hindus who formed a majority in his empire. He made significant efforts to treat them at par and soon they too were being appointed to high posts. Akbar treated religion with an extremely open mind and spent a lot of time studying the various beliefs of the different religions. This eventually resulted in the creation of a new religion of his own called Din-I-illahi . This combined features from various religions and stressed on the idea of that regardless of what religion you follow, God is one. Being a supreme believer in universal tolerance, Akbar made no attempt to force people to convert to his religion but tried to appeal to the inner feelings of each person.

Akbar's last years brought great grief to him. A beloved friend and notable poet Faizi died in 1595. Akbar's son Salim (later to be known as Jehangir) eager to take over the throne set himself up as an independent king and began plotting to overthrow Akbar.

Salim caused much pain to his father when he got another close friend and poet, Abul Fazl murdered. Father and son spent the last couple of years see- sawing between peace and war but finally after Akbar died a natural death, Salim succeeded to the throne. Akbar was a great person and a great king.

During his time the country reached a level of prosperity it had not seen and would not see for a long time. Being an able statesmen, he set an example for the other leaders that would follow.

CHAPTER TWO

Ch : 2 Akbar Life Summary

- Ch : 2 Akbar Life Summary

Emperor Akbar, also known as Akbar the Great or Jalaluddin Muhammad Akbar, was the third emperor of the Mughal Empire, after Babur and Humayun. He was the son of Nasiruddin Humayun and succeeded him as the emperor in the year 1556, when he was only 13 years old. One of the most successful emperors of the Mughal Empire, Akbar also made significant contribution in the field of art.

Apart from commencing a large collection of literature, he also commissioned a number of splendid buildings during his reign. This biography of King Akbar will provide you more information on his life history:

- Early Life

Akbar was born on 15th October 1542, to Emperor Humayun and his recently wedded wife, Hamida Banu Begum. The Rajput Fortress of Umarkot in Sind, where Humayun and Hamida were taking refuge, became the birthplace of this great emperor.

In 1540, Humayun was forced into exile by Afghan leader Sher Shah and Akbar spent his childhood in Afghanistan, at his uncle Askari's place. His youth was spent in running and fighting, rather than learning to read and write. However, this could never impair his interest in art, architecture, music and literature.

Humayun recaptured Delhi in the year 1555, with the help of his Persian ally Shah Tahmasp. However, a few months after his victory, he met with an accident and died. On 14th February 1556, Akbar succeeded the throne, in the midst of a war waged by Sikandar Shah for the Mughal throne.

- Early Rule

The first battle fought by Akbar was against Sikandar Shah Suri of Punjab. However, when Akbar was busy leading assault against Sikandar Shah, Hemu, a Hindu warrior, launched an attack on Delhi, which was then under the regency of Tardi Beg Khan. Tardi fled from the city and Hemu claimed the capital. On the advice of his general, Bairam, Akbar launched an attack on Delhi and reclaimed the city. On 5th November 1556, 'Akbar the Great' fought the Second Battle of Panipat against General Hemu.

Following soon after was the battle with Sikandar Shah at Mankot. In 1557, Adil Shah, who was the brother of Sikandar, died in a battle in Bengal. Along with fighting against the other rulers, Akbar also solidified his support by revoking the jizya tax on non-Muslims.

At the same time, he started wooing the favor of the powerful Rajput caste, at times by marrying Rajput princesses. He expanded the Mughal Empire by including Malwa, Gujarat, Bengal, Kabul, Kashmir and Kandesh, amongst others. In no time, the rule of Akbar was firmly established over the entire Hindustan (India).

- Final Years

Akbar was greatly troubled in the last few years of his life due to the misdemeanors of his sons. Especially his third son, Salim, was frequently in rebellion against his father. The last conquest of Akbar comprised of Asirgarh, a fort in the Deccan. Thereafter, he faced the rebellion of his son and breathed his last on 12th October 1605. His body was entombed in a magnificent mausoleum at Sikandra city, near Agra.

- Navratnas

1. Akbar's court had Navaratnas (Nine Jewels), meaning a group of nine extraordinary people. They included:
2. Abul Fazel (Akbars's chief advisor and author of Akbarnama)
3. Faizi (Akbar's poet laureate)
4. Mian Tansen (a Hindu singer who converted to Islam)
5. Birbal (a noble known for his wittiness)

6. Raja Todar Mal (Akbar's finance minister)
7. Raja Man Singh (trusted general of Akbar)
8. Abdul Rahim Khan-I-Khana (a noble and a renowned poet)
9. Fakir Aziao-Din
10. Mullah Do Piaza

CHAPTER THREE

Ch : 3 9 gems of Akbar

- Ch : 3 9 gems of Akbar

1. Abul Fazl (1551–1602) was the chronicler of Akbar's rule. He authored the biographical Akbarnama. Abul Fazl documented the history meticulously, over seven years, in three volumes, the third volume is known as the Ain-i-Akbari and a Persian translation of the Bible. He was also the brother of Faizi, the poet laureate of emperor Akbar.

2. Faizi (1547–1595) was Abul Fazl's brother. He was a poet who composed beautiful poetry. His father was Mubarak Nagori, a scholar in the philosophy and literature of Greece as well as in Islamic theology.

3. Miyan Tansen was a singer for King Akbar, born as Tanna Mishra, a Hindu Brahmin, in 1520, he was a poet himself. He learnt music from Swami Haridasand later from Hazrat Muhammad Ghaus. He was a court musician with the prince of Mewar and later was recruited by Akbar as his court musician. Tansen became a legendary name in India and was the composer of many classical ragas. He was an extraordinarily gifted vocalist, known for a large number of compositions, and also an instrumentalist who popularized and improved the rabab (of Central Asian origin). He was buried in Gwalior, where a tomb has been constructed for him. It is unclear if Tansen converted to Islam.

4. Raja Birbal (1528–1583) was a poor Hindu Brahmin who was appointed to the court of Akbar for his intelligence, and became the court jester. Born by the name Maheshdas, he was conferred the name Raja Birbal by the Emperor. Birbal's duties in Akbar's court were mostly military and administrative but he was also a very close friend of the emperor, who liked Birbal most for his wit and humor. There are many witty stories of exchanges and interactions between the monarch and his minister that are

popular today. Birbal was also a poet and his collections under the pen name "Brahma" are preserved inBharatpur Museum. Raja Birbal died in battle, attempting to quell unrest amongst Afghani tribes in Northwest India.

5. Raja Todar Mal was a Hindu Khatri/Kayastha and was Akbar's finance minister, who from 1560 onwards overhauled the revenue system in the kingdom. He introduced standard weights and measurements, revenue districts and officers. His systematic approach to revenue collection became a model for the future Mughals as well as the British. Raja Todar Mal was also a warrior who assisted Akbar in controlling the Afghan rebels in Bengal. Todar Mal had developed his expertise in Sher Shah's employment. In 1582, Akbar bestowed on the raja the title Diwan-I-Ashraf.

6. Raja Man Singh was the Kacchwaha Rajah of Amber, a state later known as Jaipur. He was a trusted general in Akbar's army and was the grandson of Akbar's father-in-law. His family had been inducted into Mughal hierarchy as amirs (nobles). Raja Man Singh was the foremost ablest among Akbar's military commanders and assisted Akbar in many fronts including holding off advancing Hakim (Akbar's half-brother, a governor of Kabul) in Lahore. He was also the Mughal viceroy of Afghanistan, led campaigns in Bihar, Orissa, Deccan and was also the viceroy of Bengal.

7. Abdul Rahim Khan-I-Khana was a poet was the son of Akbar's trusted protector and caretaker when he was a teenager, Bairam Khan. After Bairam Khan was murdered treacherously, his wife became the second wife of Akbar. He is most known for his Hindi couplets and his books on Astrology. The village of Khankhana, named after him, is located in the Nawanshahr district of the state of Punjab in northwest India.

8. Fakir Aziao-Din was a mystic and an advisor. Akbar regarded his advice in high esteem.

9. Mullah Do Piaza was a advisor to Akbar.

CHAPTER FOUR

Ch : 4 How Akbar meet Birbal?

- Ch : 4 How Akbar meet Birbal?

Akbar loved hunting and used to escape to go for hunting even from his studies. Well, later he became a better rider and hunter than any one of his courtiers. One day when Akbar went for hunting, he and his some of the courtiers went so fast that they left the others behind. As the evening fell, everybody got very hungry and thirsty, they found that they had lost their way and now did not know where to go.

At last they came to a junction of three roads. King was very happy to see the roads that now he could go reach his capital through one of these roads, but which road was to go to his capital - Agra. They were all thinking about it and could not decide it.

In the mean time they saw a young boy coming along one road. The boy was summoned and Akbar asked him, "Hey young boy! Which road goes to Agra?" The boy smiled and spoke, "Huzoor, everybody knows that road cannot move so how these roads can go to Agra or anywhere else?" and laughed at his own joke.

Everybody was silent, didn't say a word. The boy said again, "People travel, not the roads. Do they?" Emperor laughed at this and said, "No, you are right." The Emperor asked again, "What is your name, young boy?" "Mahesh Das" The boy replied and asked the Emperor, "And who are you Huzoor? What is your name?" The Emperor took out his Ring and gave it to the boy.

"You are talking to Emperor Akbar - the King of Hindustaan (India). We need fearless people like you. You come to the court, with this Ring I will recognize you immediately. Now tell me the way to get to Agra. We have to reach there soon?"

Mahesh Das bowing lowly pointed towards the road going to Agra, and the King headed on that road.That is how the Emperor Akbar met the future Birbal.

CHAPTER FIVE

Ch : 5 The Well Dispute

- Ch : 5 The Well Dispute

Once there was a complaint at King Akbar's court. There were two neighbours who shared their garden. In that garden, there was a well that was possessed by Iqbal khan. His neighbour, who was a farmer wanted to buy the well for irrigation purpose.

Therefore they signed an agreement between them, after which the farmer owned the well. Even after selling the well to the farmer, Iqbal continued to fetch water from the well. Angered by this, the farmer had come to get justice from King Akbar. King Akbar asked Iqbal the reason for fetching water from the well even after selling it to the farmer.

Iqbal replied that he had sold only the well to the farmer but not the water inside it. King Akbar wanted Raja Birbal who was present in the court listening to the problem to solve the dispute. Birbal came forward and gave a solution.

He said " Iqbal, You say that you have sold only the well to the farmer. And you claim that the water is yours. Then how come you can keep your water inside another person's well without paying rent?" Iqbal's trickery was countered thus in a tricky way. The farmer got justice and Birbal was fairly rewarded.

CHAPTER SIX

Ch : 6 Back to Square One

- Ch : 6 Back to Square One

As usual a lot of people were present in Akbar's durbar.A famous astrologer had come from a far away country.He was talking about the Solar System and the Earth's shape.

At one point Akbar said, "If the earth is round, and if one travel strait towards one direction, he will come back to the same spot from where he has started the journey."

"Theoretically it is correct", said the astrologer."Why not in real life?", asked the king."One has to cross oceans, mountains and forests to keep the path straight." the astrologer said. "Sail through the oceans, make tunnels in the mountains and use elephants to cross the forests." Akbar found the solution.

"Still it is impossible" said the astrologer."Why?" Asked Akbar."It may take years to complete the whole journey" said the astrologer"Years? How many?" asked Akbar."I don't know. May be a hundred years or more" said the astrologer

"Don't worry I will ask my ministers. They have an answer for everything" Akbar looked at the ministers."Impossible to calculate""Around 25 years""Fifty years or less""80 days""Why Birbal, you haven't uttered a word" the king showed his surprise at Birbal's silence.

"I was just calculating the time required to go round the earth" explained Birbal."And did you get the answer?" asked the king."Sure." Said Birbal "It will take just one day.""Just one day! Birbal it is Impossible! Even it will take more than one day to cross our country." Said Akbar."It is possible. Provided you travel at the speed of the Sun" said Birbal with a smile.

Ch : 7 The True King

Ch : 7 The True King

The King of Iran had heard that Birbal was one of the wisest men in the East and desirous of meeting him sent him an invitation to visit his country.

In due course, Birbal arrived in Iran. When he entered the palace he was flabbergasted to find not one but six kings seated there. All looked alike. All were dressed in kingly robes. Who was the real king?

The very next moment he got his answer. Confidently, he approached the king and bowed to him."But how did you identify me?" the king asked, puzzled.

Birbal smiled and explained: "The false kings were all looking at you, while you yourself looked straight ahead. Even in regal robes, the common people will always look to their king for support."Overjoyed, the king embraced Birbal and showered him with gifts.

CHAPTER EIGHT

Ch : 8 The Sharpest Shield and Sword

- Ch : 8 The Sharpest Shield and Sword

A man who made spears and shields once came to Akbar's court.

"Your Majesty, nobody can make shields and spears to equal mine," he said. "My shields are so strong that nothing can pierce them and my spears are so sharp that there's nothing they cannot pierce."

"I can prove you wrong on one count certainly," said Birbal suddenly."Impossible!" declared the man."Hold up one of your shields and I will pierce it with one of your spears," said Birbal with a smile.

CHAPTER NINE

Ch : 9 The Sadhu

- Ch : 9 The Sadhu

Akbar came to the throne when he was only thirteen years old. In the years that followed, he built on of the greatest empires of his time. He lived in unimaginable splendor.

He was surrounded by courtiers who agreed with every word he said, who flattered him and treated him as if he were a god. Perhaps it was not surprising that Emperor Akbar was sometimes arrogant and behaved as if the whole world belonged to him.

One day, Birbal decided to make the great emperor stop and think about life.

That evening as the emperor was going towards his palace, he noticed a Sadhu lying in the centre of his garden. He could not believe his eyes.

A strange Sadhu, in ragged clothes, right in the middle of the palace garden? The guards would have to be punished for this, thought the emperor furiously as he walked over to that Sadhu and prodded him with the tip of his embroidered slipper.

"Here, fellow!" he cried. "What are you doing here? Get up and go away at once!"

That Sadhu opened his eyes. Then he sat up slowly. "Huzoor," he said in a sleepy voice. "Is this your garden, then?"

"Yes!" cried the Emperor. "This garden those rose bushes, the fountain beyond that, the courtyard, the palace, this fort, this empire, it all belongs to me!"

Slowly that Sadhu stood up. "And the river, Huzoor? And the city? And this country?""Yes, yes, it's all mine", said the emperor. "Now get out!""Ah", said the Sadhu. "And before you, Huzoor. Who did the garden and fort and city belong to then?"

"My father, of course", said the emperor. In spite of his irritation, he was beginning to get interested in the Sadhu's questions. He loved philosophical discussions and he could tell, from his manner of speaking, that the Sadhu was a learned man.

"And who was here before him?" the Sadhu asked quietly."His father, my father's father, as you know."

"Ah", said the Sadhu. So this garden, those rose bushes, the palace and the fort all this has only belonged to you for your lifetime. Before that they belonged to your father, am I right? And after yours time they will belong to your son, and then to his son?

"Yes", said the Emperor Akbar wonderingly."So each one stays here for a time and then goes on his ways?""Yes."

"Like a dharmashala?" the Sadhu asked. "No one owns a dharmashala. Or the shade of a tree on the side of a road. We stop and rest for a while and then go on. And someone has always been there before us and someone will always come after we have gone. Is that not so?"

"It is", Emperor Akbar quietly.

"So your garden, your palace, your fort, your empire... these are only places you will stay in for a time, for the span of your lifetime. When you die, they will no longer belong to you. You will go, leaving them in the possession of someone else, just as your father did and his father before him."

Emperor Akbar nodded. "The whole world is a dharmashala", he said slowly, thinking very hard. "In which we mortals rest awhile. That's what you are telling me, isn't it? Nothing on this earth can ever belong to a single person, because each person is only passing through the earth and must die one day?"

The Sadhu nodded solemnly. Then, bowing to the ground, he removed his white beard and saffron turban and his voice changed. "Jahanpanah, forgive me!" he said, in his normal voice. "It was my way of asking you to think about..."

"Birbal, oh, Birbal!" the emperor exclaimed. "You are wiser than any philosopher. Come, come at once to the royal chamber and let us discuss this further. Even emperors are but wayfarers on the path of life, it is clear!"

CHAPTER TEN

Ch : 10 The Musical Genius

Ch : 10 The Musical Genius

Famous musicians once gathered at Akbar's court for a competition.The one who could capture a bull's interest was to be declared the winner.One by one, they played the most heavenly music but the bull paid no attention.

Then Birbal took the stage. His music sounded like the droning of mosquitoes and the mooing of cows.But to everyone's amazement the bull suddenly became alert and began to move in a lively manner.

Akbar declared Birbal the winner.

CHAPTER ELEVEN

Ch : 11 The Loyal Gardener

- Ch : 11 The Loyal Gardener

One day Akbar was stumbled on a rock in his garden while taking a stroll. He was not in a good mood already, and then this fall made him very angry.He ordered for the gardener's arrest and execution.

Gardener was very scared and Birbal comes to know about this episode. He met the Gardener in the prison and told him something in his ear.

The next day, at the time of execution, the gardener was asked what his last wish was. He requested for an audience with the Emperor. His wish was granted and he was brought in the Court. When he came near the throne, he loudly cleared the throat and spat at the feet of the Emperor. The Emperor demanded to know why did he do such a thing. Suddenly Birbal stepped forward in the gardener's defense.

He said, "There could be no person more loyal than this unfortunate gardener. Fearing that you ordered him for hanging for a small reason, he went out of his way to give you a genuine reason for ordering him to be hanged."

The Emperor realized his mistake and set him free.

CHAPTER TWELVE

Ch : 12 The Jealous Courtiers

- Ch : 12 The Jealous Courtiers

King Akbar was very fond of Birbal. This made a certain courtier very jealous. Now this courtier always wanted to be chief minister, but this was not possible as Birbal filled that position.

One day Akbar praised Birbal in front of the courtier. This made the courtier very angry and he said that the king praised Birbal unjustly and if Birbal could answer three of his questions, he would accept the fact that Birbal was intelligent. Akbar always wanting to test Birbals wit readily agreed.

The three questions were

1. How many stars are there in the sky

2. Where is the centre of the Earth and

3. How many men and how many women are there in the world.

Immediately Akbar asked Birbal the three questions and informed him that if he could not answer them, he would have to resign as chief minister.

To answer the first question, Birbal brought a hairy sheep and said .There are as many stars in the sky as there is hair on the sheep's body. My friend the courtier is welcome to count them if he likes.

To answer the second question, Birbal drew a couple of lines on the floor and bore an iron rod in it and said this is the centre of the Earth, the courtier may measure it himself if he has any doubts.

In answer to the third question, Birbal said Counting the exact number of men and women in the world would be a problem as there are some specimens like our courtier friend here who cannot easily be classified as either. Therefore if all people like him are killed, then and only then can one count the exact number.

CHAPTER THIRTEEN

Ch : 13 Full Moon, Quarter Moon

- Ch : 13 Full Moon, Quarter Moon

Once Birbal went to Persia at the invitation of that country's King. Parties were extended in his honor and rich gifts heaped up near him. On the eve of his departure to home, a nobleman asked him as how he would compare the king of Persia with his own King. Birbal said - "Your King is the full Moon, whereas mine could be like a quarter Moon." The Persians got very happy to hear this analogy.

Now Birbal got home and he found that Emperor Akbar was furious with him. He demanded angrily - "How could you belittle your own king? You are a traitor." Birbal said politely - "No, Your Majesty, no. I cannot belittle you. What I said there meant - "The Full Moon diminishes and disappears onward, while the quartered Moon grows gradually day by day. What I, in fact, wanted to tell the world that your power is growing day by day while the King of Persia's is about to decline now."

Akbar grunted in satisfaction and welcomed Birbal back from his journey with a warm embrace.

CHAPTER FOURTEEN

Ch : 14 The Choice of Birbal

- Ch : 14 The Choice of Birbal

One day Emperor Akbar asked Birbal what he would choose if he were given a choice between justice and a gold coin.

"The gold coin," said Birbal. Akbar was taken aback.

"You would prefer a gold coin to justice?" he asked, incredulously.

"Yes Jahaanpanaah," said Birbal.

The other courtiers were also amazed by Birbal's display of idiocy. For years they had been trying to discredit Birbal in the emperor's eyes but without success and now the man had gone and done it himself. They could not believe their good fortune.

"I would have been dismayed if even the lowliest of my servants had said this," continued the Emperor. "But coming from you? It's. . . it's shocking - and sad. I did not know you were so debased!"

"One asks only for what one does not have, Your Majesty." said Birbal, quietly. "You have seen to it that in our country justice is available to everybody. So as the justice is already available to me also; and as I'm always short of money I said I would choose the gold coin."

The emperor was so pleased with Birbal's reply that he gave him not only one but a thousand gold coins.

CHAPTER FIFTEEN

Ch : 15 The Blind Saint

Ch : 15 The Blind Saint

There lived a blind saint in an ashram in the kingdom of Emperor Akbar.He was believed to prophecy the future correctly.Once he had a visitor who had come to treat their niece. The child's parents were killed in front of the girl's eyes. Once she saw the saint, she started to scream loudly saying that that saint was the culprit.

Angered by the girl's words, the saint demanded the couple to get away with their child.The whole day the girl cried which made the couple to realize that the girl was not lying.Therefore, they decided to seek the help of Birbal.

Birbal consoled them and asked them to wait at the Emperor's assembly. Birbal had invited the saint to Akbar's court too.

Then in front of all the ministers he drew a sword and neared the saint to kill him. The saint in bewilderment immediately drew another sword and began to fight. Thus by this act of the saint it was proved that he wasn't blind.

Therefore, Akbar demanded to hang the culprit and rewarded the girl for her bravery for telling the truth even at the critical situation.

CHAPTER SIXTEEN

Ch : 16 Question for Question

- Ch : 16 Question for Question

One day Akbar asked Birbal, "Birbal, can you tell me how many bangles are on your wife's hand?" Birbal said, "No, Huzoor, I cannot." "You cannot? Although everyday you see her hand, still you cannot tell how many bangles are on her hand. How is that?" said Akbar.

Birbal said, "Let's go to the garden, Your Majesty. And I will tell you "How is that" and they both went to the garden. They both went down a small staircase which led to the garden. After reaching in the garden Birbal asked, "You daily climb up and down this small staircase, could you tell how many steps it has?"

Akbar smiled and then changed the subject.

Ch : 17 Birbal Imagination

Ch : 17 Birbal Imagination

Once Akbar told Birbal 'Birbal, make me a painting. Use imagination in it.To which the reply was 'But hoozoor, I am a minister, how can I possibly paint?'The king was angry and said 'If I don't get a good painting by one week then you shall be hanged!'The clever Birbal had an idea.

After one week, he went to the court and with him he carried a covered frame.Akbar was happy to see that Birbal had obeyed him, until he opened the cover. The courtiers rushed to see what was wrong. What they saw made them feel very happy.

At last, they would not see Birbal in court! The painting was nothing but ground and sky. There were a few specs of green on the ground.The Emperor, angrily, told Birbal 'what is this?' To which the reply was 'A cow eating grass hoozoor!'

Akbar said 'where is the cow and grass?' and Birbal told 'I used my imagination. The cow ate the grass and returned to its shed!'Akbar started laughing hearing that. As Birbal again pulled a fast on him. He rewarded him for using his intelligence.

Ch : 18 Noble Beggar

- Ch : 18 Noble Beggar

One day the Emperor asked Birbal, "Birbal, is it possible to be the both "noblest" and the "lowest" together?" Birbal said, "Yes, Jahaanpanaah" "Then bring me such a person."

Birbal went and returned next day with a beggar and presenting him to Akbar said, "This is the lowest among all of your subjects, Jehanpanah" Akbar asked, "Good, that may be true, but I don't see that how he can be the noblest?"

"He has been given the honor of having an audience with the Emperor, that makes him the noblest among the beggars, Jahaapanaah."

CHAPTER NINETEEN

Ch : 19 List of blinds

- Ch : 19 List of blinds

Once King Akbar questioned Birbal if he knows the number of blind citizens of their kingdom.Birbal had requested Akbar to give him a week's time.The next day Birbal was found to be mending shoes in the town market. People were astonished to see Birbal doing such work. Many of them started to question "Birbal!! What are you doing?"

Once when he was asked this question by someone he started writing something. It continued for a week when on the 7th day King Akbar himself asked Birbal the same question.

Giving him no answer, Birbal reported at the court the next day and handed over a note to King Akbar. Akbar read the note when he found that it was the big list of people who were blind.

Emperor Akbar was stunned when he found his own name in the list. Angered by this, Akbar asked Birbal the reason for writing his name in the list.

Birbal said "O! My majesty! Like all other people you also saw me mending the slippers but you still asked me what I was doing. Therefore I had to include your name too."

Akbar started laughing at this and everyone enjoyed Birbal's sense of humor.

CHAPTER TWENTY

Ch : 20 Just One Question

- Ch : 20 Just One Question

One Day a scholar came to the court of Emperor Akbar and challenged Birbal to answer his questions and thus prove that he was as clever as people said he was.

He asked Birbal: "Would you prefer to answer a hundred easy questions or just a single difficult one?"

Both the emperor and Birbal had had a difficult day and were impatient to leave."Ask me one difficult question," sad Birbal."Well, then, tell me," said the man, "which came first into the world, the chicken or the egg?"

"The chicken," replied Birbal."How do you know?" asked the scholar, a note of triumph in his voice."We had agreed you would ask only one question and you have already asked it" said Birbal and he and the emperor walked away leaving the scholar gaping.

CHAPTER TWENTY-ONE

Ch : 21 Birbal, can you Identify The Guest

- Ch : 21 Birbal, can you Identify The Guest

Once Birbal was invited for dinner by a rich man. When Birbal reached there, he found himself in a large crowd. The host greeted him warmly and took him inside. Birbal said, "I did not know that there will be so many guests in this gathering." The host replied politely, "They are not guests, Sir. They are my employees except one who is the only other guest here besides you. Could you tell who is that other one guest here?"

"Maybe, I could. Tell them a joke, and I will observe them." The rich man told the joke and everybody laughed uproariously. Perhaps this was the worst joke Birbal had ever heard in his life. Now the rich man asked Birbal, "I have told the joke, now you tell me who is the other guest here?" Birbal pointed out towards a man and said, "He is that other guest." The rich man was very surprised hearing this that how could he recognize the other guest. He said to him, "You are right Birbal, but how did you recognize him?"

Birbal said, "Because only employees can laugh on such a joke. He was the only person who did not even smile on your joke, so I immediately recognized him as the other guest."

CHAPTER TWENTY-TWO

Ch : 22 Cooking The Khichdi

- Ch : 22 Cooking The Khichdi

On a cold winter day Akbar and Birbal took a walk along the lake. A thought came to Birbal that a man would do anything for money. He expressed his feelings to Akbar. Akbar then put his finger into the lake and immediately removed it because he shivered with cold.

Akbar said "I don't think a man would spend an entire night in the cold water of this lake for money."Birbal replied "I am sure I can find such a person."Akbar then challenged Birbal into finding such a person and said that he would reward the person with a thousand gold coins.

Birbal searched far and wide until he found a poor man who was desperate enough to accept the challenge. The poor man entered the lake and Akbar had guards posted near him to make sure that he really did as promised.

The next morning the guards took the poor man to Akbar. Akbar asked the poor man if he had indeed spent the night in the lake. The poor man replied that he had. Akbar then asked the poor man how he managed to spend the night in the lake. The poor man replied that there was a street lamp near by and he kept his attention affixed on the lamp and away from the cold.

Akbar then said that there would be no reward as the poor man had survived the night in the lake by the warmth of the street lamp. The poor man went to Birbal for help.

The next day, Birbal did not go to court. The king wondering where he was sent a messenger to his home. The messenger came back saying that Birbal would come once his Khichri was cooked. The king waited hours but Birbal did not come. Finally the king decided to go to Birbal's house and see what he was upto.

He found Birbal sitting on the floor near some burning twigs and a bowl filled with Khichri hanging five feet above the fire. The king and his attendants couldn't help but laugh. Akbar then said to Birbal "How can the Khichri be cooked if it so far away from the fire?"

Birbal answered "The same way the poor man received heat from a street lamp that was more than a furlong away."

The King understood his mistake and gave the poor man his reward.

Ch : 23 Birbal Turns Tables

- Ch : 23 Birbal Turns Tables

Once Emperor Akbar was narrating his dream in the court. The dream began with Akbar and Birbal walking towards each other on a dark night. It was so dark that they could not see each other, and so collided and fell. The Emperor said - "Fortunately for me, I fell into a sea of Paayzam (an Indian sweets made with milk and semolina), but guess what Birbal fell into?" Courtiers asked curiously - "What, Your Majesty?"

"A gutter." The whole court resounded with laughter. The Emperor was thrilled that at least for once he had been able to score over Birbal.

But Birbal was unperturbed. As the laughter had died down, he said - "Your Majesty, Strangely enough, I too had the same dream, but unlike you I slept on till the end. When you climbed out of that pool of delicious Paayazam, and I climbed out of that stinking gutter, we found that there was no water with which to clean ourselves and so guess what we did?" Asked the Emperor - "What did we do, Birbal?" Birbal said smilingly - "We licked each other to clean each other."

The Emperor got red with embarrassment and resolved never to let Birbal down again.

CHAPTER TWENTY-FOUR

Ch : 24 Birbal The Wise Man

- Ch : 24 Birbal The Wise Man

In the town of Agra there lived a rich businessman. But he was also quite a miser. Various people used to flock outside his house everyday hoping for some kind of generosity, but they always had to return home disappointed. He used to ward them off with false promises and then never live up to his word.

Then one day, a poet named Raidas arrived at his house and said that he wanted to read out his poems to the rich man. As the rich man was very fond of poetry, he welcomed him in with open arms.

Raidas started to recite all his poems one by one. The rich man was very pleased and especially so when he heard the poem that Raidas had written on him, because he had been compared with 'Kubera', the god of wealth. In those days it was a custom for rich men and kings to show their appreciation through a reward or a gift, as that was the only means of earning that a poor poet possessed. So the rich man promised Raidas some gifts and asked him to come and collect them the next day. Raidas was pleased.

The next morning when he arrived at the house, the rich man pretended that he had never laid eyes on him before. When Raidas reminded him of his promise, he said that although Raidas was a good poet he understood very little of human nature.

And that if rich businessman truly wanted to reward him, he would have done so the very same night. Raidas had been offered a reward not because he was really pleased or impressed, but to simply encourage him.

Raidas was extremely upset, but as there was nothing that he could do, he quietly left the house. On his way home he saw Birbal riding a horse. So he stopped him and asked for his help after narrating the whole incident.

Birbal took him to his own house in order to come up with a plan. After giving it some thought he asked Raidas to go to a friend's house with five gold coins and request the friend to plan a dinner on the coming full moon night, where the rich man would also be invited. Birbal then asked Raidas to relax and leave the rest to him.

Raidas had one trustworthy friend whose name was Mayadas. So he went up to him and told him the plan.. The next day, Mayadas went to the rich man's house and invited him for dinner.

The dinner has been planned for the coming full moon night. He said that he intended to serve his guests in vessels of gold, which the guests would get to take home after the meal. The rich man was thrilled to hear this and jumped at the offer.

After sunset on the full moon night, the rich man arrived at Mayadas' house and was surprised to see no other guests there but Raidas. Anyhow, they welcomed him in and started a polite conversation. The rich man had come on an empty stomach and so was getting hungrier by the minute. Raidas and Mayadas were quite full as they had eaten just before the rich man's arrival.

Finally at midnight the rich man could bear his hunger no longer and asked Mayadas to serve the food. Mayadas sounded extremely surprised when he asked him what food was he talking about. The rich man tried to remind him that he had been invited for dinner. At this point Raidas asked him for proof of the invitation.

The rich man had no answer. Then Mayadas told him that he had just invited him to please him and had not really meant it. He then went on to say that even though they did not do anything good for other people they also would never try to hurt another human being. He asked the rich man not to feel bad.

At that point Birbal walked into the room and reminded the rich man of the same treatment that he had himself meted out to Raidas. The rich man realised his mistake and begged for forgiveness. He said that Raidas was a good poet and had not asked him for any reward.

He himself had promised to give him some gifts and then cheated him out of them. To make up for his mistake he took out the necklace that he was wearing and gifted it to Raidas.

Then they all sat down to eat a happy meal.

Raidas was all praise for Birbal and thanked him profusely. Emperor Akbar also invited him to his court and honoured him, all thanks to Birbal.

Birbal really was a wise man.

Ch : 25 Neither here nor there

- Ch : 25 Neither here nor there

The wisdom of Birbal was unparalleled during the reign of Emperor Akbar. But Akbar's brother-in-law was extremely jealous of him. He asked the Emperor to dispense with Birbal's services and appoint him in his place. He gave ample assurance that he would prove to be more efficient and capable than Birbal. Before Akbar could take a decision on this matter, this news reached Birbal.

Birbal himself resigned and left. Akbar's brother-in-law was made the minister in place of Birbal. Akbar decided to test his new minister. He gave three hundred gold coins to him and said, "Spend these gold coins such that, I get a hundred gold coins here in this life; a hundred gold coins in the other world and another hundred gold coins neither here nor there."

Now the minister found the entire situation to be a maze of confusion and hopelessness. He spent sleepless nights worrying over how he would get himself out of this mess. Thinking in circles was making him go crazy. Eventually, on the advice of his wife he sought Birbal's help. Birbal said - "Just give me the gold cons. I shall handle the rest."

Akbar's brother-in-law had no choice so he gave all the coins to Birbal. Birbal walked the streets of the city holding the bag of gold coins in his hand. He noticed a rich merchant celebrating his son's wedding. Birbal gave a hundred gold coins to him and bowed courteously saying - "The Emperor Akbar sends you his good wishes and blessings for the wedding of your son. Please accept the gift he has sent." The merchant felt honored that the king had sent a special messenger with such a precious gift. He honored Birbal and gave him a large number of expensive gifts and a bag of gold coins as a return gift for the king.

Next, Birbal went to the area of the city were the poor people lived. There he bought food and clothing in exchange for a hundred gold coins and distributed them in the name of the Emperor.

When he came back to town he organized a concert of music and dance. He spent a hundred gold coins on it.

The next day Birbal entered Akbar's court and announced that he had done all that the king had asked his brother-in-law to do. The Emperor waited to know how he had done it.

Birbal repeated the sequences of all the events and then said - "The money I gave to the merchant for the wedding of his son – you have got back while you are living on this earth. The money I spent on buying food and clothing for the poor – you will get it in the other world. The money I spent on the musical concert – you will get it neither here nor there."

CHAPTER TWENTY-SIX

Ch : 26 Birbal Gave Birth to the Child

- Ch : 26 Birbal Gave Birth to the Child

Once somebody had a wound in the palace of the Emperor. The royal Vaidya was called and he suggested that if the milk of a camel is applied on the wound, it will be cured soon. The Emperor announced it in his court that he needed camel's milk. Everybody was surprised to hear this but could not say anything.

A couple of days passed but nobody could find camel's milk. So Birbal was assigned this work. Birbal tried his best to explain to the Emperor that there is no such thing like camel's milk, but he said - "When Raaj Vaidya has asked for it, it must exist. Bring it from anywhere." Birbal got very upset. He went home and thought how to tell the Emperor that there is no such thing like camel's milk.

Thinking this a couple of days passed and Birbal did not go to the court also. Akbar got worried what has happened to Birbal? He sent somebody to his house to see why he did not come the court.

When he went there, he met his daughter washing Birbal's clothes just outside the house.

She greeted the servant. The servant asked her - "What happened Birbal has not come to the court?" The daughter replied - "Last night Birbal had a child." The servant could not digest this statement but he came back and told this to the Emperor. The Emperor also could not understand this, so he himself decided to to his house and find out the truth.

Seeing the Emperor coming Birbal greeted him. The Emperor asked him - "Birbal, What is this? Can a man give birth to child?"Birbal politely replied

- "Huzoor, When a camel can have milk, why can't a man give birth to a child?"The Emperor understood that he was caught unaware. He returned to his palace and cancelled his orders.

CHAPTER TWENTY-SEVEN

Ch : 27 Birbal's Sweet Reply

- Ch : 27 Birbal's Sweet Reply

Akbar used to ask many odd questions from his courtiers and amused himself. One day he entered the Royal Court, settled in his Royal chair, and asked his courtiers:

"What punishment should be given to a person who pulls my mustache?"One said, "He should be beheaded."Another said, "He should be flogged."Yet another said, "He should be hanged."

"What do you think, Birbal?" the Emperor asked Birbal. Birbal kept quiet for a moment, then said, "Jahaanpanaah, he should be given sweets."What, Birbal? Have you gone crazy? Do you know what are you saying?"

Birbal replied politely, "I am not crazy, Jahaanpanaah. And I know what I am saying."Then how can you talk like this?" the King asked in anger. Birbal again replied politely, "Because, Jahaanpanaah, the only person who can dare to do this is your grandson."

Akbar was so pleased with this answer, that he gave his ring to Birbal as a reward.

CHAPTER TWENTY-EIGHT

Ch : 28 Birbal Shortens Road

- Ch : 28 Birbal Shortens Road

Once the Emperor Akbar was traveling to a distant place along with some of his courtiers. It was a hot day and the Emperor was tired of his journey. He asked querulously - "Can't any shorten this road for me?" Birbal said - "Yes, I can." The other courtiers looked at one another perplexed. All of then knew that there was no other path through the hilly terrain.

The road on which they were traveling, was the only one that could take them to destination. So they were surprised to hear Birbal that he could shorten the road.

The Emperor said - "You can shorten the road? Well, do it." Birbal said - "I will." And he started - "Listen to to this story I will tell you now." And riding beside the Emperor's palanquin, he started telling him a long story that held Akbar and all others listening to it attentively and spellbound. They had arrived at their destination before they could think anything else.

Exclaimed Akbar - "Oh, we have reached, Birbal. So soon?" Birbal grinned - "Well, That is what you wanted - the road to be shortened."

CHAPTER TWENTY-NINE

Ch : 29 Birbal's Generosity

- Ch : 29 Birbal's Generosity

One day a man stopped Birbal in a street and began narrating his woes to him. He said finally - "I have walked 20 miles to see you, and all along the way people kept saying that you are the most generous man in the country."

Birbal knew that the man is going to ask some money from him. He asked - "Are you going back the same way?" The man replied - "Yes Sir." Birbal said - "Will you do me a favor?" The man said "Certainly, why not? What do you want me to do?"

Birbal said - "Please deny the rumor of my generosity all the way back to your home." And Birbal walked away.

CHAPTER THIRTY

Ch : 30 How Birbal Brought Meat Back in the Community?

- Ch : 30 How Birbal Brought Meat Back in the Community?

Akbar was famous for his religious tolerance. (Jodhaa Baaee, a Hindu woman, was his wife, he had married other religion's women also) He would help to all those who wanted help even on religious matters.

Once it so happened that a group of Braahman appeared in his court and said - "O Great Emperor, You are the one who allowed us to ask you if we had problems. We have stayed silent for long time, but today we wish to speak up. We do not want any slaughtering of animals, it is against our religion."

Hearing this Akbar got in a fix as the meat was the most important food in the market. He couldn't think of anything else except to call Birbal and ask his help in this matter. After thinking for a while, Birbal offered his solution, he said - "Your request can be granted on two conditions; one, that if any animal was found on the road, we are not responsible for his safety; two, that all animals should be fed in houses till their death, if any animal was found eating something outside, we are not responsible for his safety also."

Braahman went back happily. A month went by. The same Braahman again appeared in the court and said - "O Jahaanpanaah, We take our words back, we cannot keep our animals inside."

That is how Birbal brought meat back in the community.

CHAPTER THIRTY-ONE

Ch : 31 Birbal Is Brief

- Ch : 31 Birbal Is Brief

One day Akbar asked his courtiers if they could tell him the difference between truth and falsehood in three words or less.

The courtiers looked at one another in bewilderment."What about you, Birbal?" asked the emperor. "I'm surprised that you too are silent."I'm silent because I want to give others a chance to speak," said Birbal."Nobody else has the answer," said the emperor. "So go ahead and tell me what the difference between truth and falsehood is — in three words or less."

"Four fingers" said Birbal"Four fingers?" asked the emperor, perplexed.

"That's the difference between truth and falsehood, your Majesty," said Birbal. "That which you see with your own eyes is the truth. That which you have only heard about might not be true. More often than not, it's likely to be false."

"That is right," said Akbar. "But what did you mean by saying the difference is four fingers?"The distance between one's eyes and one's ears is the width of four fingers, Your Majesty," said Birbal, grinning.

Ch : 32 Colorful Bird

- Ch : 32 Colorful Bird

Akbar was very fond of birds. One day a bird catcher came to his kingdom . He had a very colorful bird. The Bird catcher said to Emperor Akbar that this bird is not only colorful like a peacock, but it can dance also like him and also fly. The Bird catcher was immediately rewarded with 50 gold coins. He left the kingdom in a hurry.

When the bird catcher had gone Birbal said to Emperor - "This bird cannot dance like a peacock and it has not bathed for many months." Birbal further suggested - "Let me give it a bath." and asked for a glass of water.

When Birbal gave the bath to the bird, everybody was surprised to see that it was not any special bird but was actually a pigeon and the bird catcher had fooled every body by painting it. Its color was coming out in water.

Everybody asked Birbal that how did he know this. Birbal told that he saw colors on the nails of the bird catcher. The bird catcher was caught and given a punishment. The reward that was given to the bird catcher was now given to Birbal.

CHAPTER THIRTY-THREE

Ch : 33 Washerman's Donkey

- Ch : 33 Washerman's Donkey

Once Akbar went to the river with his two sons and wise Minister Birbal. On the bank of the river, Akbar and his two sons took off their clothes and asked Birbal to take care of them while they took bath in the river.

Birbal was waiting for them to come out of the river. All the clothes were on his shoulder. Looking at Birbal standing like this, Akbar felt like teasing him, so he said to him, "Birbal, you look like as if you are carrying a washerman's donkey load."

Birbal quickly retorted, "Sir, Washer-man's donkey carries only one donkey's load, I am carrying three donkey's load." Akbar was speechless.

CHAPTER THIRTY-FOUR

Ch : 34 Birbal Identifies Thief

- Ch : 34 Birbal Identifies Thief

It so happened that once a rich merchant's house was robbed. The merchant suspected that the thief was one of his servants. So he went to Birbal and mentioned the incident. Birbal went to his house and assembled all of his servants and asked that who stole the merchant's things. Everybody denied.

Birbal thought for a moment, then gave a stick of equal length to all the servants of the merchant and said to them that the stick of the real thief will be longer by two inches tomorrow. All the servants should be present here again tomorrow with their sticks.

All the servants went to their homes and gathered again at the same place the next day. Birbal asked them to show him their sticks. One of the servants had his stick shorter by two inches. Birbal said, "This is your thief, merchant."

Later the merchant asked Birbal, "How did you catch him?" Birbal said, "The thief had already cut his stick short by two inches in the night fearing that his stick will be longer by two inches by morning."

CHAPTER THIRTY-FIVE

Ch : 35 Akbar's Hasty Judgement

- Ch : 35 Akbar's Hasty Judgement

Once the Emperor Akbar was riding near a mango grove. An arrow whizzed past him. His soldiers rushed to the grove and caught the person who did this. He was a young boy. On asking why did he want to kill the Emperor, he said that he did not want to kill the Emperor, he just wanted to knock down a mango from a high branch.

The Emperor was too angry to listen to him. He ordered to put him to death in the same way as the boy wanted to kill him.

A soldier tied the boy with a tree stump and steadied his arrow to kill him. Birbal, who was watching all this process quietly so far, now shouted, "This is not fair. If you want to shoot him in the same way as he tried to shoot the Emperor, then you will have to aim for a mango. And then the arrow has to miss the mango and strike the boy."

Akbar had calmed down by now. Thinking that it was unfair to the boy, he ordered his soldiers to release the boy. Thus Birbal saved that innocent boy.

CHAPTER THIRTY-SIX

Ch : 36 Quick Thinking Birbal : Count The Crows

- Ch : 36 Quick Thinking Birbal : Count The Crows

One day Akbar was strolling in his palace gardens with his dear minister Birbal. Many crows were flying around. The King enjoyed their flying. Just then he thought, that how many crows could be in his kingdom and immediately posed this question to Birbal.

Birbal thought a moment, then said, "They are ninety-five thousand, four hundred and sixty three (95, 463) crows in your kingdom, Huzoor." "How do you know that for sure?" the King asked. "You can get them counted, Huzoor." Birbal said.,

The king again said, "If there will be less than that, then?" Birbal replied immediately, "That means that the rest of them have gone on vacation to some neighboring kingdoms." "Or if there were more than that, then?" "Then it means that other crows are visiting your kingdom, Huzoor."

CHAPTER THIRTY-SEVEN

Ch : 37 Hot Iron Test

- Ch : 37 Hot Iron Test

One day, one man wanted to punish a man named Hasan. He accused him of stealing his necklace, and reported this theft in the police. The case was brought in the Judge's court. Judge knew Hasan very well, and he also knew that he was not a thief.

So he asked the man, "Why do you think that Hasan has stolen your necklace?" The man replied, "Your Honor, I have seen him stealing the necklace." Hasan said, "I am innocent, Your Honor. I do not know anything about his necklace."

The man then said, "All right, if he is innocent, let him prove his innocence. let me bring the hot iron, and if he can hold it in his bare hands, then I will agree that he has not stolen my necklace, and he is speaking truth."

The man said, "It means that if I am speaking the truth, then I will not burn my hands with that red hot iron?" "Yes, you are right. God will protect you."

Now Hasan could not do anything but to hold red hot iron in his hands to prove his innocence, and that he was speaking the truth. He asked judge to give him one day to look for that necklace again. The judge gave him permission. He went home.

He took advice from Birbal. He returned next day he came back and said, "I am ready for that, Sir, if you think so. But the same thing should apply to him too. If he is speaking the truth, then the red hot iron should not burn his hands also. So let him bring that red hot iron holding in his both hands, then I will hold that iron in my bare hands."

Now the man was speechless. He told the Judge that he would go and search his necklace again in his house, maybe it was misplaced somewhere there, bowed hastily and went away.

CHAPTER THIRTY-EIGHT

Ch : 38 The Cock and the Hen

- Ch : 38 The Cock and the Hen

Since Birbal always outwitted Akbar, Akbar thought of a plan to make Birbal look like a fool. He gave one egg to each of his ministers before Birbal reached the court one morning.

So when Birbal arrived, the king narrated a dream he had had the previous night saying that he would be able to judge the honesty of his ministers if they were able to bring back an egg from the royal garden pond.

So, Akbar asked all his courtiers to go to the pond, one at a time and return with an egg. So, one by one, all his ministers went to the pond and returned with the egg which he had previously given them.

Then it was Birbal's turn. He jumped into the pond and could find no eggs. He finally realized that the King was trying to play a trick on him. So he entered the court crowing like a cock.

The Emperor asked him to stop making that irritating noise and then asked him for the egg.Birbal smiled and replied that only hens lay eggs, and as he was a cock, he could not produce an egg.Everyone laughed loudly and the King realized that Birbal could never be easily fooled.

CHAPTER THIRTY-NINE

Ch : 39 The Wicked Barber's Plight

- Ch : 39 The Wicked Barber's Plight

As we all know, Birbal was not only Emperor Akbar's favourite minister but also a minister dearly loved by most of the commoners, because of his ready wit and wisdom. People used to come to him from far and wide for advise on personal matters too.

However, there was a group of ministers that were jealous of his growing popularity and disliked him intensely. They outwardly showered him with praise and compliments, but on the inside they began to hatch a plot to kill him.

One day they approached the king's barber with a plan. As the barber was extremely close to the king, they asked him to help them get rid of Birbal permanently. And of course, they promised him a huge sum of money in return. The wicked barber readily agreed.

The next time the king required his services, the barber started a conversation about the emperor's father who he also used to serve. He sang praises of his fine, silky-smooth hair. And then as an afterthought he asked the king that as he was enjoying such great prosperity, had he made an attempt to do anything for the welfare of his ancestors?

The king was furious at such impertinent stupidity and told the barber that it was not possible to do anything because they were already dead. The barber mentioned that he knew of a magician who could come of help. The magician could send a person up to heaven to enquire about his father's welfare. But of course this person would have to be chosen carefully; he would have to be intelligent enough to follow the magicians instructions as well as make on-the-spot decisions. He must be wise, intelligent and responsible. The barber then suggested the best person for the job – the wisest of all ministers, Birbal.

The king was very excited about hearing from his dead father and asked the barber to go ahead and make the arrangements immediately. He asked him what was needed to be done. The barber explained that they would take Birbal in a procession to the burial grounds and light a pyre. The magician would then chant some 'mantras' as Birbal would ascend to the heavens through the smoke. The chantings would help protect Birbal from the fire.

The king happily informed Birbal of this plan. Birbal said that he thought it a brilliant idea and wanted to know the brain behind it. When learning that it was the barber's idea, he agreed to go to heaven on condition that he be given a large some of money for the long journey as well as one month's time to settle his family so that they had no trouble while he was gone. The king agreed to both conditions.

In the duration of this month, he got a few trustworthy men to build a tunnel from the funeral grounds to his house. And on the day of the ascension, after the pyre had been lit, Birbal escaped through the concealed door of the tunnel. He disappeared in to his house where he hid for a few months while his hair and beard grew long and unruly.

In the meantime his enemies were rejoicing as they thought that they had seen the last of Birbal.

Then one day after many, many months Birbal arrived at the palace with news of the king's father. The king was extremely pleased to see him and ready with a barrage of questions. Birbal told the king that his father was in the best of spirits and had been provided with all the comforts except one.

The king wanted to know what was lacking because now he thought he had found a way to send things and people to heaven. Birbal answered that there were no barbers in heaven, which is why even he was forced to grow his own beard. He said that his father had asked for a good barber.

So the king decided to send his own barber to serve his father in heaven. He called both the barber and the magician to prepare to send him to heaven. The barber could say absolutely nothing in his own defence as he was caught in his own trap. And once the pyre was lit he died on the spot.

Nobody dared to conspire against Birbal again.

CHAPTER FORTY

Ch : 40 Akbar Birbal Reunion

- Ch : 40 Akbar Birbal Reunion

One day, when Akbar and Birbal were in discussions, Birbal happened to pass a harmless comment about Akbar's sense of humour. But Emperor Akbar was in a foul mood and took great offense to this remark. He asked Birbal, his court-jester, friend and confidant, to not only leave the palace but also to leave the walls of the city of Agra. Birbal was terribly hurt at being banished.

A couple of days later, Akbar began to miss his best friend. He regretted his earlier decision of banishing him from the courts. He just could not do without Birbal and so sent out a search party to look for him. But Birbal had left town without letting anybody know of his destination. The soldiers searched high and low but were unable to find him anywhere.

Then one day a wise saint came to visit the palace accompanied by two of his disciples. The disciples claimed that their teacher was the wisest man to walk the earth. Since Akbar was missing Birbal terribly he thought it would be a good idea to have a wise man that could keep him company. But he decided that he would first test the holy man's wisdom.

The saint had bright sparkling eyes, a thick beard and long hair. The next day, when they came to visit the court Akbar informed the holy man that since he was the wisest man on earth, he would like to test him. All his ministers would put forward a question and if his answers were satisfactory he would be made a minister. But if he could not, then he would be beheaded. The saint answered that he had never claimed to be the wisest man on earth, even though other people seemed to think so. Nor was he eager to display his cleverness but as he enjoyed answering questions, he was ready for the test.

One of the ministers, Raja Todarmal, began the round of questioning. He asked "Who is a man's best friend on earth?" To which the wise saint replied, "His own good sense". Next Faizi asked which was the most superior thing on earth? "Knowledge", answered the saint. "Which is the deepest trench in the world?", asked Abdul Fazal. And the saint's answer was "a woman's heart". "What is that which cannot be regained after it is lost?" questioned another courtier and the reply he received was 'life'. "What is undying in music" asked the court musician Tansen. The wise saint replied that it was the "notes". And then he asked "which is the sweetest and most melodious voice at night -time? And the answer he received was "the voice that prays to God."

Maharaj Mansingh of Jaipur, who was a guest at the palace asked, "what travels more speedily than the wind?" the saint replied that it was "man's thought". He then asked, "which was the sweetest thing on earth?" and the saint said that it was "a baby's smile".

Emperor Akbar and all his courtiers were very impressed with his answers, but wanted to test the saint himself. Firstly he asked what were the necessary requirements to rule over a kingdom, for which he was answered 'cleverness'. Then he asked what was the gravest enemy of a king. The saint replied that it was 'selfishness'. The emperor was pleased and offered the saint a seat of honour and asked him whether he could perform any miracles. The saint said that he could manifest any person the king wished to meet. Akbar was thrilled and immediately asked to meet his minister and best friend Birbal.

The saint simply pulled off his artificial beard and hair much to the surprise of the other courtiers. Akbar was stunned and could not believe his eyes. He stepped down to embrace the saint because he was none other than Birbal.

Akbar had tears in his eyes as he told Birbal that he had suspected it to be him and had therefore asked him whether he could perform miracles. He showered Birbal with many valuable gifts to show him how happy he was at his return.

Ch : 41 Hunting & Dowry

- Ch : 41 Hunting & Dowry

Akbar had a passion for hunting. One day Akbar was on his hunting trip, that he heard two owls quarreling very fiercely. Akbar asked Birbal, "Birbal, what are these owls saying? Why are they quarreling so loudly?"

Birbal said, "Both of them are settling the dowry amount, Huzoor. The first one who is groom's father, is saying that he wants to take 40 jungles in the dowry, with no animals at all. The other owl, who is bride's father is saying that he can arrange only 20 jungles at the moment."

In the mean time one owl hooted once more very loudly. Akbar asked Birbal, "Now what is he saying?" Birbal said, "Now he is saying that if you wait for six months more, I can give you 40 jungles without animals."

Akbar understood what Birbal wanted to say - do not kill animals, so he gave up hunting altogether.

CHAPTER FORTY-TWO

Ch : 42 Akbar's Ring

- Ch : 42 Akbar's Ring

Once Akbar went for hunting, and there his ring fell in a dry well. Now how to take that ring out. They did not have any means to take it out. Then Birbal said, "Huzoor, if you give me some time I can take your ring out of this well. Akbar had no alternative, so he permitted him.

Birbal went around and brought some fresh cow dung and threw it on the ring. He then tied a stone on one end of a string, and holding the other end in his hand threw the stone on the cow dung. He waited for a long time - for the cow dung to be dried, and then pulled the string out of the well. The string brought the stone, the stone was stuck into cow dung and the cow dung had the Emperor's ring at its bottom.

Akbar got very happy with Birbal's intelligence.

CHAPTER FORTY-THREE

Ch : 43 Fear is the key

- Ch : 43 Fear is the key

One day King Akbar said to Birbal, "Birbal, my people are very obedient to me. They love me very much." Birbal smiled and replied, "This is true, but they fear you too, Jahaanpanaah." Akbar could not agree on this, so it was decided that Birbal's statement should be tested.

Next day, according to Birbal's instructions, the King announced that he would be going for hunting, and people should pour a pot of milk in a tub kept in the courtyard. Next day when Akbar returned from hunting, he found that there was no milk in the tub, instead there was only water. Akbar got very disappointed, but couldn't do anything.

Then Birbal said, "This time you will announce that you will come back and see the tub yourself." King did as Birbal said. Once again the tub was kept in the courtyard. This time when King returned from the hunting, he found the tub overflowing with milk. Birbal said, "I told you. It is your fear which made people obey you. The first time there was no one to check the tub, so people poured the water, but the second time, they knew that you would check yourself, that is why they brought the milk."

Thank You So Much Message

For Your Supported & For Your Loves Thank You So Much. Have A Greatest Day Of Your. If I am successful today, because of my father, if he lived today, he would have been very happy, he will always and always be with me.